THIS BOOK
BELONGS TO:

_____

_____

_____

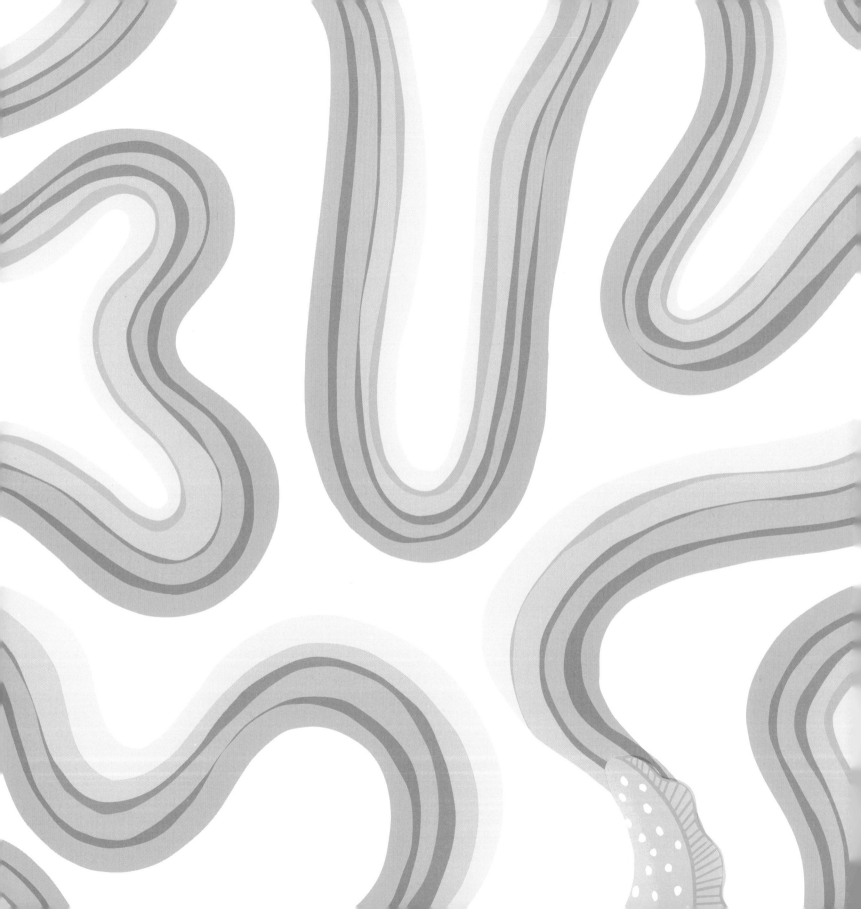

WORDS BY
SABRINA MOYLE

PICTURES BY
EUNICE MOYLE

HANG IN THERE!

ABRAMS APPLESEED
NEW YORK

Have you ever had a day
when *nothing* seems to go your way?

DOINK!

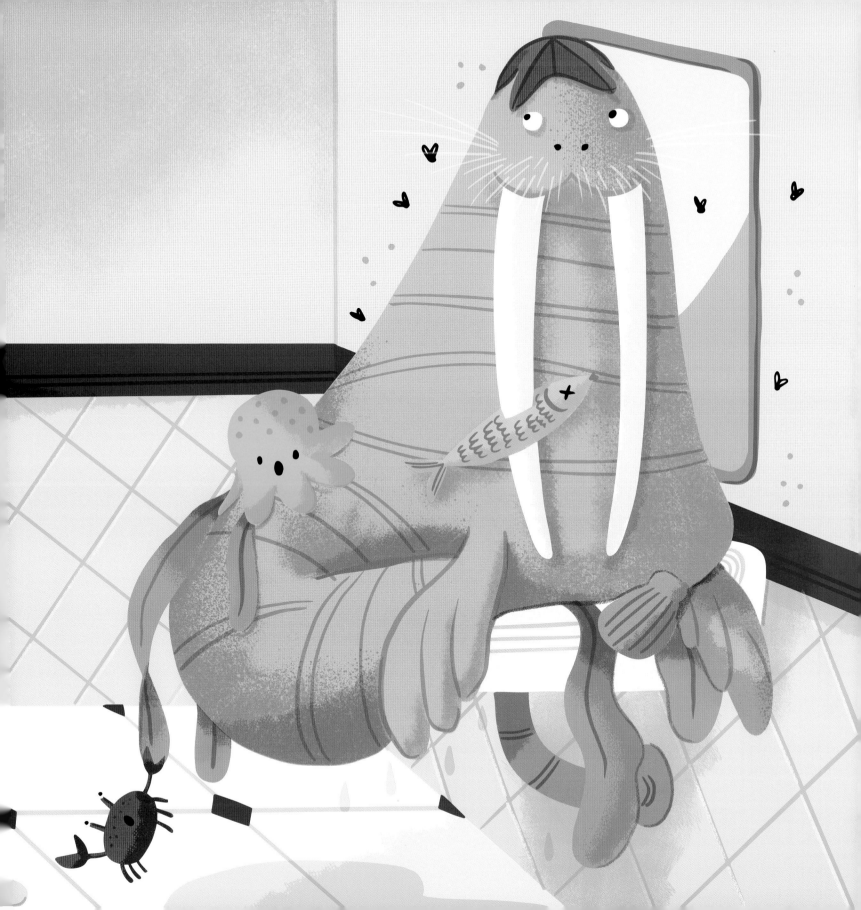

Yippee! You found your favorite shirt!
But wait. It's soaked in inky squirt.

You need to eat.
Your stomach churns.

But what's that smell?
Ew! Scrambled worms?!

Time to go. Where is your coat?
It's being eaten by a goat!

On the bus, you're feeling beat.
Wait—who's that sitting in your seat?

You're on a roll. You've got big plans.
But someone has a LOT of hands!

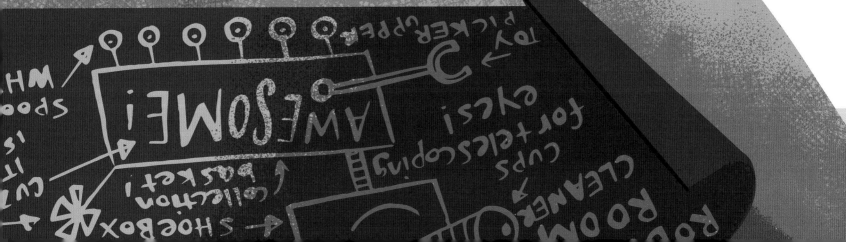

READING NOOK

You want to curl up with a book,
but there's a boa in the nook!

QUIET PURR-LEASE!

"I'm going home—you're much too loud!"

But no one hears you in the crowd.

"I've had it with this lousy day!"

You decide to go and play.

But . . .

... a yak is sitting
on your toys.

It then lets out an
awful noise.

PPPPF

This is absurd. You start to laugh.

So does the goat.
And the giraffe!

Don't give up. No, never, nope.
Where there is humor, there is hope!

We are brave birds of a feather.
We'll take this bad day on together!

So hold on, friend!
Do not despair.

When times are tough,
just hang in there!

For Charles, dear fur-end and fellow carbon-based life form —S.M.

For Daniel, my favorite purr-son —E.M.

The illustrations in this book were created digitally.

Library of Congress Control Number 2021935235
ISBN 978-1-4197-5556-9

Printed and bound in China
10 9 8 7 6 5 4 3 2 1

For bulk discount inquiries, contact specialsales@abramsbooks.com.

ABRAMS The Art of Books
195 Broadway, New York, NY 10007
abramsbooks.com